THE MOO-GIC OF MERLIN

Steve Cole

Illustrated by Woody Fox

RED FOX

THE MOO-GIC OF MERLIN
A RED FOX BOOK 978 1 862 30543 4

First published in Great Britain by Red Fox,
an imprint of Random House Children's Books
A Random House Group Company

This edition published 2009

3 5 7 9 10 8 6 4 2

Text copyright © Steve Cole, 2009
Illustrations copyright © Woody Fox, 2009

The Random House Group Limited supports the Forest Stewardship
Council (FSC), the leading international forest certification organization.
All our titles that areprinted on Greenpeace-approved FSC-certified paper
carry the FSC logo. Our paper procurement policy can be found at
www.rbooks.co.uk/environment.

Red Fox Books are published by Random House Children's Books,
61–63 Uxbridge Road, London W5 5SA

www.kidsatrandomhouse.co.uk
www.rbooks.co.uk

Addresses for companies within The Random House Group Limited
can be found at: www.randomhouse.co.uk/offices.htm

THE RANDOM HOUSE GROUP
Limited Reg. No. 954009

A CIP catalogue record for this book is available
from the British Library.

Printed and bound in Great Britain by
CPI Bookmarque, Croydon CR0 4TD

To Kit and Alex

★ THE C.I.A. FILES ★

Cows from the present —
Fighting in the past to protect the future . . .

In the year 2550, after thousands of years of being eaten and milked, cows finally live as equals with humans in their own country of Luckyburger. But a group of evil war-loving bulls — the Fed-up Bull Institute — is not satisfied.

Using time machines and deadly ter-moo-nator agents, the F.B.I. is trying to change Earth's history. These bulls plan to enslave all humans and put savage cows in charge of the planet. Their actions threaten to plunge all cowkind into cruel and cowardly chaos . . .

The C.I.A. was set up to stop them.

However, the best agents come not from 2550 — but from the present. From a time in the early 21st century, when the first clever cows began to appear. A time when a brainy bull named Angus McMoo invented the first time machine, little realizing he would soon become the F.B.I.'s number one enemy . . .

COWS OF COURAGE - TOP SECRET FILES

PROFESSOR ANGUS MCMOO

Security rating: Bravo Moo Zero

Stand-out features: Large white squares on coat, outstanding horns

Character: Scatterbrained, inventive, plucky and keen

Likes: Hot tea, history books, gadgets

Hates: Injustice, suffering, poor-quality tea bags

Ambition: To invent the electric sundial

LITTLE BO VINE
Security rating: For your cow pies only
Stand-out features: Luminous udder (colour varies)
Character: Tough, cheeky, ready-for-anything rebel
Likes: Fashion, chewing gum, self-defence classes
Hates: Bessie Barmer; the farmer's wife
Ambition: To run her own martial arts club for farmyard animals

PAT VINE
Security rating: Licence to fill (stomach with grass)
Stand-out features: Zigzags on coat
Character: Brave, loyal and practical
Likes: Solving problems, anything Professor McMoo does
Hates: Flies not easily swished by his tail
Ambition: To find a five-leaf clover — and to survive his dangerous missions!

Prof. McMoo's
TIMELINE OF NOTABLE
HISTORICAL EVENTS

4.6 billion years BC
PLANET EARTH FORMS
(good job too)

13.7 billion years BC
BIG BANG - UNIVERSE BEGINS
(and first tea atoms created)

23 million years BC
FIRST COWS APPEAR

(23 million is my lucky number!)

1700 BC
SHEN NUNG MAKES FIRST CUP OF TEA
(what a hero!)

7000 BC
FIRST CATTLE KEPT ON FARMS
(Not a great year for cows)

1901 AD
QUEEN VICTORIA DIES
(she was not a-moo-sed)

2550 BC
GREAT PYRAMID BUILT AT GIZA
(by an Egyptian geezer)

31 BC ROMAN EMPIRE FOUNDED

(Roam-Moo empire founded by a cow but no one remembers that)

1509 AD HENRY VIII COMES TO THE THRONE

(and probably squashes it)

1066 AD BATTLE OF HASTINGS

(but what about the Cattle of Hastings?)

1620 AD ENGLISH PILGRIMS SETTLE IN AMERICA

(bringing with them the first cows to moo in an American accent)

1939 AD WORLD WAR TWO BEGINS

(or World War Moo as it is known to cows)

2007 AD I INVENT A TIME MACHINE!!!

2500 AD COW NATION OF LUCKYBURGER FOUNDED

(HOORAY!)

(about time!)

1903 AD FIRST TEABAGS INVENTED

2550 AD COWS IN ACTION RECRUIT PROFESSOR McMOO, PAT AND BO

(and now the fun REALLY starts...)

THE MOO-GIC
OF MERLIN

Chapter One

CUSTARD ALERT

"Switch off those alarms!" yelled Yak Buttbuster, stomping into the C.I.A. operations room. Sirens were going off, red lights were flashing, and the big, black bull could hardly think.

Seeing the scowl on his face, Yak's staff of highly trained cows rushed to obey. Being Director of the Cows In Action, an elite band of constantly crime-busting, time-travelling cattle commandos, Yak often had plenty to scowl about. But right now he was feeling scowlier than ever. C.I.A. spies had just reported that the F.B.I. – the dreaded Fed-up Bull Institute – was committing a time-crime in one of the murkiest, most mysterious periods of Earth's history . . .

As the sirens shut off, Yak turned to his Chief Operative. "Quick, Dandi – send an alert signal to our top agents. And you'd better make it a *custard*-grade alert!"

"Yes, Director." Dandi, a plump and pleasant white cow, hit a large, yellow button. "I'll just trace the signal back through time to make sure it reaches them . . ." She switched on a large TV screen built into the wall and started fiddling with the controls. In moments, it showed a peaceful, empty field.

Yak watched eagerly. While he and his team were based in the twenty-sixth

century, his best agents lived on a small, organic farm way back in the twenty-first . . .

"No sign of them, Director," Dandi reported. "Where can they be?"

Suddenly, a blaze of purple light shone into the operations room. Staff milled about in alarm, mooing loudly.

But Yak smiled. "They're right here. It's the Time Shed!"

Sure enough, a large, ramshackle barn was appearing in the corner of the room. Built from old farm machinery and techno-junk saved from a scientist's bin, this incredible invention had helped change the course of cow history – allowing cattle to become the first ever travellers through time.

A second later, the wooden doors swung open and a reddy-brown bull with white squares patterning his hide strode out: the Time Shed's creator, Professor Angus McMoo.

"Spot on! C.I.A. headquarters in the year 2150 AD, just as I planned." McMoo beamed round at the sash-wearing cows, pushed his glasses up onto his snout and gave a jokey salute. "Kettle on, is it, Yak? I'm parched!" Despite the state of emergency, Yak couldn't help but smile. McMoo was a bull like no other. One of the bravest and most brilliant of all time, his incredible thirst for knowledge was matched only by his even more incredible thirst for tea.

"Glad you showed up," the black bull rumbled. "I've been looking for you and your friends, Professor."

A dairy cow with a rosy red-and-white coat burst from the shed behind McMoo. "And now you've found us, Yakky-baby!"

"Shhh, Little Bo," said a young, light-brown bullock with zigzags on his coat,

following her out. "Yak's very important;
you can't call him 'Yakky-baby' in front
of everybody . . ."

"You're so boring, little bruv," Bo
complained. "Besides, Yak doesn't mind
– do you, Beef-cheeks?"

Yak grimaced and tried not to blush.
Little Bo Vine was not a typical cow in
this time, her own time or any time in-
between. Like the professor and Pat, she
belonged to a rare breed of twenty-first
century clever cattle called the Emmsy-
Squares. But unlike them, this feisty
cow's hobbies were fashion, fighting and
dying her udder different colours (today
it was bright yellow).

"Sorry for barging in like this,
Director Yak," Pat went on quickly.
"You see, the professor has just finished
rewiring the Time Shed's engines—"

"So I thought I'd razz over here on
a test-drive!" said McMoo. "You won't
believe how fast we whizzed through

the twenty-third century . . ." He stared round anxiously. "You do *have* a kettle, don't you?"

"I have an emergency situation on my hooves," said Yak, as Dandi duly trotted up with a big bucket of tea for the professor. "That's why I sent out a custard alert."

Pat raised an eyebrow. "Custard alert?"

"Like a red alert, only yellow with added egg yolks and an accompanying banana," McMoo explained, between gulps of tea. "Well, a banana if you're lucky."

"We're *not* lucky," Yak declared. "As I was saying, we're on a banana-*free* custard alert because—"

"Ugh!" Bo pointed to the big TV screen and pulled a face. "That's enough to put *anyone* on alert!"

The screen showed a familiar huge, hairy figure standing in the field, like a cross between a very ugly woman and a weightlifting gibbon. Pat shuddered — it was Bessie Barmer, who ruled the farm with an iron fist, a steel boot and, most likely, rocks in her head. She hated all the animals and couldn't wait to turn them all into pies — which was why the professor had built his Time Shed in the first place, so that he, Pat and Bo could zoom away and escape danger.

Things hadn't quite worked out that way. The only thing they had zoomed into was adventure after adventure, fighting for the Cows In Action!

"Bessie Barmer is *not* the reason we're on custard alert, Bo," said Yak, starting to lose his patience. "That's just the P.O.O. scanner."

"Well, it found some *poo* all right!" said Bo.

"No, P.O.O. stands for Past Object

Observation," Dandi explained. "I was about to look for you on your farm when you showed up here!"

"Oi, husband!" Bessie yelled from the screen. "Are you still trying to get that old pickaxe out from that lump of concrete? You big wimp!"

Pat clutched his stomach. "She makes me feel ill even when I'm five hundred years away in the future!"

"I'll pull it out, easy!" Bessie boasted. "My family have links all the way back to King Arthur, that bloke who pulled the sword from the stone 'cause he was born to rule – just like me!"

Bo blew a raspberry. "She's always boasting about her famous ancestors. Somebody turn off that screen, before I'm sick."

"It's funny she should mention King Arthur,"

said Yak as Dandi turned off the P.O.O. scanner. "Arthur and his head wizard, Merlin, seem to be at the centre of the F.B.I.'s latest evil plot."

"*Plot*-ever do you mean?" McMoo drained his bucket and stared at Yak. "I thought Arthur and Merlin and Camelot were just folk tales made up in the Middle Ages – not real history."

Yak shook his head. "That's what everyone thought in *your* time. But new evidence found in *our* time has proved that many of those old stories were actually based on fact."

"Wow," breathed McMoo, and Pat smiled to see his idol look so amazed.

"Yeah, that's a real thrill." Bo yawned. "So, what's going down with this Arthur King bloke, then?"

"Our spies report that an important F.B.I. agent named Moodrid wants to use him to change history," Yak explained. "And apparently, a brand-new type of ter-moo-nator is involved . . ."

Pat shivered at the mere mention of the word. Ter-moo-nators were tough, scheming creatures — part robot, part bull — which the F.B.I often used to do their dirty work. "The old ter-moo-nators were bad enough," he said. "What will this *new* one be like?"

Bo shrugged. "What will it be like to *PUNCH*? That's what *I* can't wait to find out!"

"Well, whatever Moodrid and his mate are up to," said McMoo, "we'd better get stopping them."

Yak passed the professor a small, electronic device. "This place-date datachip has the time and destination programmed in. But take care, troops. Something tells me this mission will be

extra-dangerous . . ."

"Good!" Bo blew him a kiss and ran back into the shed. "See ya soonie, Yak-a-roonie!"

McMoo waved. "Ta for the tea! We'll be in touch soon."

"We hope!" added Pat as he followed the professor inside.

"So do I," Yak muttered. He and Dandi watched anxiously as the Time Shed blurred and vanished in a blaze of purple light – off to the Dark Age . . .

Chapter Two

DANGER IN THE DARK AGE!

McMoo loaded up the place-date datachip and started skipping gleefully about the Time Shed. The unlikely vessel's high-tech insides were a big contrast to its drab exterior. Panels

full of switches and buttons lined the wooden walls. Thick, snake-like power cables hummed with energy. A huge bank of controls shaped like a horseshoe rose up from the middle of the room and a computer screen dangled from the rafters. Several hay bales served as chairs. The only other piece of furniture was a special cupboard crammed full of costumes from all times and places, specially made to fit cows.

Pat smiled. "You seem very excited, Professor."

"How could I not be?" McMoo cried. "We're on our way to see Camelot in the year 521 AD. Imagine that!"

"What *is* Camel-Hot?" Bo wondered. "Something you get in the desert?"

McMoo was about to give a very pointed reply when the Time Shed lurched. Pink sparks shot out of a cable on the wall, and the noise of the engines dipped.

"Oops! Must be a blockage in the new power feeds. Soon have it fixed."

McMoo grabbed a screwdriver and started checking his precious engines. "While we're waiting . . . Computer. Give us the Camelot file."

++Camelot. ++Magnificent Dark Age city, said to be home to Arthur Pendragon, King of the Britons. ++Arthur and his knights met at the Round Table — round so that all positions were equal (and so it was easier to pass the salt). ++They did good deeds, went on quests, rescued damsels in distress and slew strange beasts. ++Arthur's friend and most trusted advisor was an old man named Merlin, a wizard with many mysterious powers. ++Arthur also had a magical sword called Excalibur, given to him by the supernatural Lady of the Lake. ++The blade was so bright it blinded his enemies, and its scabbard protected its wearer from harm.

"What an amazing story!" cried Pat.

"That Merlin bloke sounds dodgy," Bo declared. "He's not *really* a wizard, is he?"

"Wizards *have* been known to exist, Bo. Just look at me!" McMoo popped

up from behind the engines, covered in grease. "There. Give the boosters ten seconds to warm up and we can get off again."

Pat smiled. "Shall I get you a cloth, Professor?"

"No need." McMoo ran off to the costume cupboard. "The grease will help me squeeze into my Dark Age disguise!" He pressed some buttons on the side of the cupboard door and two spindly metal arms whizzed out. "I fixed the auto-dresser earlier, let's test it . . ."

"Ten seconds!" called Bo, keen to get going.

"Righto." The professor smiled as the auto-dresser started rummaging inside the cupboard. "Just press that big black button on the console."

Pat nudged it gingerly with his hoof —
and suddenly the Time Shed zoomed off
like a rocket! Pat and Bo yelled, clinging
on to the horseshoe of controls as the
hum of the engines rose to a fearsome
shriek . . .

Then just as suddenly, with a squeal of
brakes, the shed came to a dead stop.

"*Whoaaaaaaaa!*" yelled Pat, as he
and his sister were sent flying into the
costume cupboard. *CR-RUNCHH!*

Clothes exploded from inside, and the cupboard itself was smashed to matchwood.

Bo groaned. "Now you've fixed up the engines, Prof, how about getting some seatbelts for this thing?"

Pat raised his aching head and looked around. "Where *is* the professor?"

Even as he spoke, something stirred beneath the mound of clothes and splintered wood. The next moment, a

huge, menacing figure burst up into sight, its face a blank mask of milk-white metal, its body encased in shining, studded armour . . .

"*Argh!*" cried Pat. "It's that new top-secret ter-moo-nator!"

"Stay back, little bruv." Bo jumped up. "I'll get him!"

The ter-moo-nator shook his head frantically – but Bo was already kicking out with both her back legs. *CLANG!* Her hooves struck the figure right in the chest and it collapsed with a crash of clanking metal.

"*Ow!*" came a very familiar voice from inside the armour.

Bo looked at Pat. "Whoops!"

Pat gulped. "Professor?"
The figure wrenched
off its helmet — and
sure enough, Pat and
Bo saw McMoo's
miffed face looking
back at them.

"I know you meant well, Bo — but
unfortunately, you also *bent* well!"
McMoo held up an assortment of
flattened metal pieces. "You knocked
me into the suit of armour that Pat was
going to wear!"

Pat sighed as he helped up the
professor. "I would have loved to have
been a knight, too."

"Sorry, bruv," said Bo. "But I hope *my*
suit of armour isn't squashed!"

McMoo cleared his throat as he
crossed to check his controls. "Er . . . I'm
afraid there weren't any girl knights."

Pat grinned. "They were too busy
being damsels in distress."

"Yuck! I'm not being a damsel in distress for anyone." Bo stooped to grab a gauntlet from the pile of clothes. "Look, this metal glove is still OK. I can wear it on my udder!" She went on rummaging through the heap of fashions. "Do you think it goes with this cape?"

"Forget the clothes for now," said McMoo. "That sudden spurt of speed might have blown the controls. We'd better see if we've pitched up in the right place." He slipped a silver nose ring – a ringblender – through his snout. This brilliant C.I.A. device projected an optical illusion that made cows look like humans and translated all languages too. "There!" He put his helmet back on, ran over to the doors and threw them open. "If we bump into anyone they'll see me as a human knight, and you two as normal cows."

"*Normal?*" Pat looked at the metal glove hanging down from Bo's belly and the black cape round her neck. "Her?"

Bo ignored him as she followed the professor from the shed on all fours. "Hey, it's dark out here."

"Well, it is the *Dark* Age," McMoo reminded her.

Pat poked out his nose. The air was crisp and fresh. A full moon shone down from the night sky, its light splashing silver over peaceful countryside. The shed had landed in a large field ringed by low hills. To the east loomed the first sentinel-like trees of a spooky forest, while in the distance to the north Pat could see the impressive ramparts of a walled city. Towering above the walls was a magnificent castle, festooned with turrets and banners, its white stonework aglow in the moonlight.

"That must be Camelot!" cried McMoo. "We *have* arrived in the right place. Just think, the real Merlin and King Arthur live in there . . ."

Pat nodded, staring in wonder — when suddenly a rough sack was brought down over his head! "Hey!" he yelled, as strong hands grabbed hold of him and tried to bundle him away. "Get off!"

"What d'you think you're playing at?" Bo hollered — and Pat realized she must have been attacked too. He heard angry human voices, but without a ringblender, he couldn't understand them. Likewise, he knew that humans would hear anything he and Bo said only as a series of moos.

McMoo, however, was wearing *his* ringblender. "Stand back, peasants!" he commanded. "How dare you attack these cows?" Then he gasped. "Oh, no. Not *YOU* . . ."

Frantically, Pat pulled free of the

sweaty, clutching hands and shook off the sack — to find himself face to face with his enormous, boil-ridden, flabby-cheeked attacker. It was a woman. But not just any woman.

She looked exactly like the Fury of the Farmyard herself — Bessie Barmer!

Chapter Three

A WIZARD BULL

Professor McMoo glared at the woman, and the bald, burly man standing beside her. "Stop your moaning, tin-head!" the Bessie lookalike growled. "These cows *want* to come back with me to my lovely butcher's shop . . ."

"They do not! Leave them alone," said McMoo. "Can't you see I'm a knight?"

"Can't *you* see that I'm Bessivere Barmer, the master butcher?" the woman retorted. "And that my husband Henry here has a very big meat cleaver?"

Henry held up the broad blade, which gleamed in the moonlight. "Hurr, hurr!"

McMoo narrowed his eyes. "Pat, Bo, get back beside me."

"She's one of Bessie's annoying ancestors, isn't she?" Pat panted, backing away.

"We meet them wherever we go," Bo agreed crossly.

"Quick, take these." McMoo passed them each a ringblender. "Without proper clothes you'll still look like cattle — but at least you'll be able to understand the local lingo . . ."

Bessivere gave McMoo a funny look. "Are you talking to those cows?"

"It's more fun than talking to unpleasant peasants," McMoo retorted. "How dare you attack my friends!"

"Because *my* friends are staying over tonight, and they need feeding!" Bessivere scowled. "Since that rotten wizard Merlin went funny, all the cattle for miles around are holed up in Camelot. No one's so much as sniffed a bit of beef in weeks! And as you're not even carrying a sword, you can't stop us helping ourselves . . ."

"Hurr! Hurr!" laughed Henry, advancing with his cleaver.

With a defiant *moo*, Bo reared up and fired a supersonic squirt of milk. The gauntlet

jammed over her udder was forced
flying through the air like a hefty metal
fist! It struck Henry right in the face
and sent him tumbling into Bessivere,
who collapsed in a screeching heap of
quivering arms and legs.

Thinking fast, Pat whipped off Bo's
cape and flung it over the would-be
butchers.

McMoo grinned. "That covers
that, then!"

"Wait!" demanded a very royal voice behind them. "What is going on here?"

The C.I.A. agents whirled round to find a grand-looking man behind them on a magnificent white horse. A dark shaggy bull with remarkably long horns and a dark blanket over his back stood on all fours beside him.

"Oh, no!" Bessivere groaned. "It's K-K-K-King Arthur . . . and Merlin!"

McMoo noticed the crown perched on the man's head and the proud spirit shining in his eyes. "Greetings, sire!" he cried, bowing quickly, with a wary nod to the bull. "But, er . . . where *is* Merlin?"

"Are you blind, good Sir Knight?" Arthur smiled. "Merlin is right here!"

To McMoo's amazement, the big, brown bull stood and placed a tall, pointed wizard's hat on his head – and as he did so, the "blanket" on his back was revealed to be a flowing purple cape decorated with moons and stars. "Sorry, I dropped my hat," the bull said, his eyes sparkling a deep-sea green. "Yes, *I* am Merlin!"

While Bessivere and Henry started bowing and scraping, McMoo swapped incredulous glances with Pat and Bo.

"The computer never said that Merlin was a bull," Pat whispered.

"It said he was an old man," Bo agreed. "That's got to be a ter-moo-nator – or an F.B.I. agent at the very least. How could anyone believe in a man turning into a bull?"

"This is an age of superstition," McMoo reminded her. "The people believe in all kinds of miracles. But I'm not so sure I do!"

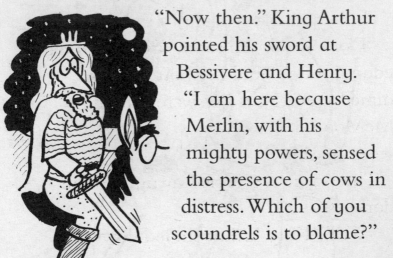

"Now then." King Arthur pointed his sword at Bessivere and Henry. "I am here because Merlin, with his mighty powers, sensed the presence of cows in distress. Which of you scoundrels is to blame?"

Henry giggled nervously and looked at Bessivere. "Hurr! Hurr!"

"It probably *was* her, Your Majesty," McMoo put in. "Henry here is too stupid to do anything for himself!"

"Thank you, Sir Knight. Well then, be off with you, peasants!" cried Arthur. "And if I ever hear of you menacing cattle again, I'll put you in the stocks and have you pelted with cowpats, do you understand?"

"Thank you, most merciful Majesticalness," said Bessivere, curtseying badly and dragging Henry away. "Thank you for sparing us the cowpats."

"Don't speak too soon," Bo murmured, edging round until her bottom was aimed squarely at Bessivere – until McMoo noticed and gave her a warning shove.

The Barmers scurried away into the darkness.

"Well!" King Arthur smiled down at

McMoo. "Now that those yucky yokels have gone, who are you, and what is your business?"

"I am, er . . . Sir Angus," said McMoo. "My cow is called Bo and my bullock is Pat. We have come because men say that Camelot is a safe place for all cattle, and cow safety is my number one concern." He looked hard at Merlin. "Speaking of which . . . aren't you supposed to be an old man with a long white beard?"

"I was, once." Merlin smiled sadly. "But what does outward appearance matter? I wear this form in anticipation of a coming battle . . ."

"Oh, yes?" McMoo raised his eyebrows. "Tell me more."

"Later," King Arthur declared. "Sir Angus, will you and your cattle accompany me to my castle, where we can feast, talk in comfort and celebrate the safety of two more cows?"

McMoo looked at Pat and Bo. "Perfect chance to check out the place," he murmured, "and Merlin's story at the same time." He turned back to King Arthur. "You're on, sire — lead on to Camelot!"

King Arthur shook his head. "It is Camelot no longer, Sir Angus. These days I call it . . . *Cow-me-lot!*"

Whatever its name, Pat decided that King Arthur's walled city was quite remarkable.

He and Bo walked on all fours behind the professor, still pretending to be ordinary, unclever cows. Led by

the king on horseback with Merlin
the mysterious bull at his side, they
entered through an enormous cobbled
courtyard. It was filled with cattle,
munching on mounds of grass in the
moonlight. While trumpets blared and
noblemen hailed the return of their king,
Pat helped himself to a few mouthfuls of
the yummy greenery.

Bo nudged up beside him. "I think we
should clobber Merlin now and make
him tell us what's going on."

"But what if he really *is* a wizard?"

said Pat cautiously. "He might turn us
into frogs or something!"

"The old myths do say that Merlin
could change his shape," McMoo noted.
"Perhaps they weren't *myth*-taken!" He
winked at his two friends. "Come on,
keep up – and let's watch old Moo-lin
closely!"

Pat, Bo and McMoo followed the
royal procession from the courtyard
on to winding, well-lit streets. They
passed market stalls and cathedrals,
smoky taverns and ornamental gardens.

All around them cows and people milled together happily under the stars.

"An F.B.I. agent would never let ordinary cows have such a nice time," Pat hissed to his sister. "He'd be trying to make them savage and bad."

"If you ask me, it's a trick," Bo grumbled.

"I say! WAIT!" came a booming voice. Pat and Bo tensed themselves as a handsome nobleman rushed up to them. But all he did was lay down his fine, velvet cloak over a tiny puddle in the street ahead of them.

"There, my noble cattle! Now you may cross safely and in comfort."

Bo gave him a funny look. Pat mooed politely to say thank you.

King Arthur glanced back at McMoo.

"Do you approve of Cow-me-lot, Sir Angus?"

"Yes, it's very nice," the professor replied. "But tell me, Your Majesty – why is everyone so crazy about cattle here?"

"We are kind to cows because Merlin had a dread vision of approaching evil," Arthur explained.

"Oh?" McMoo turned to Merlin. "And what might this approaching evil be?"

"A beautiful heifer came to me in my dreams," the wizard proclaimed. "She revealed that an evil federation of fed-up bulls is fast approaching from a land far-off . . . led by the sinister sorcerer, Moodrid." Merlin's green eyes glittered. "It is my destiny to battle Moodrid . . . and if I cannot defeat him, the whole world is doomed!"

Chapter Four

A KNIGHT TO REMEMBER

Pat and Bo stared at each other in amazement. "How does he know about the F.B.I.?" Pat whispered.

Bo nodded. "Even about Moodrid!"

"You are very well informed, Merlin," McMoo remarked.

The bull-wizard smiled thinly. "The heifer in my vision was very precise."

"But how did you change into a bull?" the professor persisted.

"Magic!" said King Arthur.

"Or rather, *moo*-gic," Merlin corrected him. "When I awoke from my vision, I found myself transformed. It can only be the work of this Moodrid . . ."

"But, come, my friends," said King Arthur. "The street is no place for such a conversation. Let us go to my castle, and talk in comfort in the Round Stable."

McMoo frowned. "Don't you mean, 'Round *Table*'?"

"No, 'Stable'," Arthur insisted. "We have quite a few cows sleeping there at the moment!"

As Merlin padded onwards, McMoo drew closer to King Arthur. "Sire . . . are you certain that is the *real* Merlin?"

"I have known Merlin all my life," the king declared. "That bull has all Merlin's memories, the same mastery of magic . . . the same eyes, even." Arthur chuckled as he, McMoo, Pat and Bo all set off again.

"Besides, turning into a bull is quite
normal behaviour by Merlin's standards!
Once, when I was a child, he became a
huge dark stag with a white forefoot . . ."

The Round Stable was located in the keep of King Arthur's castle. As Merlin led the way inside, Pat saw it was indeed a large, circular stable. The flagstones were littered with straw, and a round table sat in the middle, surrounded by several dozing cows. While he and Bo had to make do with a place on the floor, McMoo jumped in a chair and swung his hooves onto the table, grinning from ear to ear.

"I still don't see why you're keeping so many cows here in Camelot," said the professor. "Cow-me-lot, I mean."

Merlin parked his huge hindquarters on a stool. "The heifer in my vision told me that the fed-up bulls plan to turn cows against people . . . To smite down humans and give savage cows the right of rule!"

"Sounds like them," Pat agreed quietly.

"So Merlin had the most *wizard* idea!" Arthur declared. "He told me to decree that all knights must treat cows with the utmost care and respect and that no one in the land must be allowed to eat them. That will make the cows happy – and why should *happy* cows ever turn against us?"

"He's got a point," Bo whispered to Pat.

"And yet, I remain in this bullish form," said Merlin, his green eyes troubled. "Perhaps I must stay this way until Moodrid and his moo-gic are finally defeated."

"Never fear, Merlin," said Arthur. "We shall go on rescuing cows until you're back as the scrawny, bearded old magician we know and love!" He clapped his wizard heartily on the back,

and bowed down to Pat
and Bo. "And now, let
us feast in thanks for
our two new guests.
I shall order my
servants to fetch food
and drink from the
nearest tavern . . . Bye
for cow — er, *now*, I
mean!" With a cheery
wave, Arthur dashed
from the stable.

Merlin shuffled off the chair.
"Alas, I am too worn out to feast. I
think I will retire to my private rooms."
The wizard adjusted his hat, got stiffly
back onto all fours and walked away.
"Farewell, Sir Angus."

McMoo waved, as Pat watched the
wizard go. "He left in a bit of a hurry."

"That bull is bogus," Bo declared. "I
bet he's got rid of the real Merlin. He
must be an F.B.I. agent!"

"There's something fishy going on,"
McMoo agreed. "Or *bully*, anyway
– so we'd better watch him. Bo, come
with me. Pat, you stay here – so Arthur
knows I'll be coming back."

"Be careful!" Pat called as Bo and the
professor charged out of the stable. Then
he settled down among the snoozing
cows to wait.

The night air felt cool against Bo's hide
as she ran out into a deserted Cow me-

lot courtyard and scanned the area. "There's Merlin, Professor!" she hissed, jabbing a hoof towards a fancy turret.

McMoo nodded – he could see the wizardly bull yawning at the window. "That tower must be where he lives," he murmured. "Let's see what he's up to . . ."

They ran to the turret, and started climbing the torch-lit stairs to Merlin's private rooms. But as they neared the landing, they heard a heavy door creak open in the shadows.

The next moment, a figure dressed in a monk's robes appeared in front of them at the top of the stairs. With a sudden chill, Bo saw two yellow eyes glowing in the darkness of its face . . .

McMoo gasped. "It's a ter-moo-nator!"

Chapter Five

VANISHING ACT

Little Bo reared up and raised her fists. "Don't worry, Professor — I'll flatten it!"

With a grind of gears, the metal monster retreated back towards Merlin's chambers. It seemed taller and slimmer than any ter-moo-nator Bo had met before.

"Quick!" McMoo shouted. "Don't let it get away!"

Bo was already off and charging along the dark stone landing in hot pursuit. A heavy wooden door slammed shut in front of her. Without hesitating, she launched into a flying kung-moo kick, ready to smash the old wood to smithereens . . .

But just as she was about to crash through the door, it was suddenly yanked open!

"*Whoa!*" yelled Bo. With nothing in her path she went whizzing into the wizard's chambers and banged into a massive pile of books, scrolls and manuscripts. Pages went flying and dust clouded into the air as she tumbled to the stone floor in a heap.

Winded and gasping for breath, Bo realized the ter-moo-nator must have opened the door – it was standing with one hoof still on the handle, rocking with silent laughter.

"Laugh about *this*, metal mush!" Bo hurled one of the heavy books at the ter-moo-nator, conking it right on its hooded head. The robotic creature reeled backwards and crashed against the wall.

As it did so, something fell from beneath its robes, clattering to the floor.

The next moment, McMoo rushed inside. "Bo! Are you all right?"

"Behind you, Professor!" Bo yelled, struggling up from the dusty pile of papers.

McMoo turned in time to catch the full brunt of a mechanical punch to the stomach. Although his armour protected him from the worst of the blow, he was still knocked to the floor – while the robed ter-moo-nator escaped back onto the landing.

"Ahhh!" McMoo cried.

"Professor!" Bo crawled over to join him. "Are you hurt?"

"No, I'm fascinated. Look at this!" He showed her a magnificent silver sword lying on the floor. A cow's head had been carved into the hilt, with green jewels pressed into the eyes. "This design is far too sophisticated for the Dark Age . . ."

"I heard the ter-moo-nator drop it just now." Bo snatched the sword. "Let's stick this right up its big, metal—"

"First we have to catch the thing." McMoo scrambled up and hared back out onto the landing. "I didn't hear it clanking off down the stairs."

"So it must be up here still somewhere," she growled, waving the sword at the shadows. "Come out, you miserable lump of techno-beef. There's nowhere to hide!"

But apparently there was. Bo soon came to the end of the landing, and it was empty.

McMoo ran to join her. "Strange. How did that ter-moo-nator get away?" He glanced back at the open door behind him. "And where's Merlin? How come he didn't come out to investigate the noise?"

"Hang on," said Bo, pointing to a small metal box in the shadowy corner of the landing. "What's this?"

McMoo crouched to see. "It looks like an F.B.I. transporter device," he whispered.

"How does it work?" wondered Bo. She prodded it with the point of the sword – and the metal box hummed into life, glowing with fierce, red energy.

"It works like that!" McMoo yelled. "Must be programmed to respond to F.B.I. technology. Get back—"

But it was too late. In the wink of

an eye, both Bo and the professor
disappeared ...

"Come on, guys," muttered Pat
nervously inside the Round Stable.
"King Arthur's going to be back at any
moment ..."

"Here I am, Sir Angus!" cried Arthur,
bursting in. "I ran into my old friend Sir
Percival and brought him to say hello ..."

A plump, red-haired knight pushed
past the king. "Look at me! I'm Sir
Percival!"

"And *we* are Sir Percival's catering staff!" cheered four more men, struggling into the room with huge trays laden with fine-smelling food and wine. They plonked the lot down on the Round Table.

"Hooray!" shouted Sir Percival, grabbing a piece of pie and looking about. "But . . . where's this new boy, Arthur?"

King Arthur frowned and glanced at Pat. "He can't be far away. He left one of his cows."

But then, Merlin the bull barged in, his wizard's hat wedged wonkily on one horn, a frantic look in his eyes. "Sire!" he cried. "I have—"

"Have you seen Sir Angus anywhere?" Arthur interrupted.

"Eh?" Merlin seemed taken aback. "No, I thought he was here."

Arthur considered. "Perhaps he has gone exploring."

Perhaps, thought Pat, frowning.

"Never mind Sir Angus, sire – I've just had another vision!" Merlin straightened his tall hat. "The heifer of my dreams – she came to me once more in my bedchamber!"

Sir Percival stared. "Did she?"

"And she gave me a message," Merlin went on, eyes bright. "You must go to Dozmary Pool, Arthur. And when you do, you will learn of a marvellous quest.

A quest that will occupy the knights of
the Round Stable for many years . . .
A quest that will bring happiness to all
cows, and save the world!"

"A quest!" Sir Percival beamed. "It's
been *weeks* since I went on a good
quest!"

"A quest that is good for cows *and*
will save the world?" Arthur jumped in
the air and downed a large cup of ale.
"Hooray!"

"HOORAY!" The catering staff joined in with the excitement, dancing a little jig – until one of them accidentally dropped a vol-au-vent on the floor and his friends told him off for spoiling the mood.

Arthur and Sir Percival strode heroically from the stable, and Merlin followed them outside. Pat gulped. Had the moo-gical warlock done something to Bo and the professor? Were the bull's visions just a load of bull? The young C.I.A. agent knew there was only one way to find out. Silently, stealthily, Pat set off after them . . .

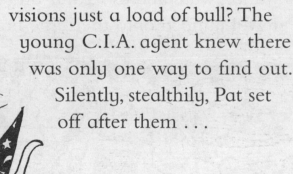

Chapter Six

DISCOVERED!

Pat peeped out from behind a cart in the courtyard near Cow-me-lot's entrance, watching as Arthur and Sir Percival jumped onto their fine horses.

Arthur's white steed had been fitted with a special carriage daubed with moons and stars, which Merlin climbed into with some difficulty. *Arthur accepts everything his wizard tells him*, Pat realized. *He might be the man in charge – but Merlin is the power behind the throne . . .*

The drawbridge creaked open, and the regal riders galloped away into the night. Pat charged after them as fast as he could. Luckily, towing Merlin in the carriage meant that Arthur's horse couldn't go too fast, and Sir Percival kept pace with him. So Pat followed them from what he hoped was a safe distance, tramping over moonlit fields, scrambling through streams and picking a path through scraps of forest. He only hoped that Bessivere Barmer wasn't still roaming about with her horrible husband.

Finally, from the brow of a moonlit hill, a dark, eerie stretch of water ringed with reeds and bulrushes came into sight. Behind it stood a thick wood.

"Here we are!" cried Sir Percival, slowing his stallion. "Dozmary Pool."

King Arthur glanced back at Merlin. "Do we need to gather at any particular part of the lake?"

Merlin peered out from his carriage. "We must go down to the water's edge . . ."

Pat watched the three of them descend the hill. Then he made his own way down in a different direction. If he could sneak round to the far side of the lake, he could spy on them from the cover of the rushes.

Keeping low, Pat started to circle the still, black waters. Then his hoof caught on something soft. He crouched to see.

It was a robe. The sort a monk would wear. "What would a monk be doing swimming out here at night-time?" Pat wondered aloud. Then he noticed a

black sack, half hidden by rushes at the lake's edge. There was a label on the side. PLEASE DO NOT STEAL. PROPERTY OF TER-MOO-NETTE 1-1-ALPHA. Pat felt a shiver go through him. "What's a ter-moo-nette?"

Something long, dark and pointed was poking out from inside the sack. Pat reached in and pulled out a well-crafted sword from a finely made scabbard. Carved into the silver hilt was a cow's face with glowing green eyes. As Pat touched the scabbard, his hoof tingled as if with some strange energy. He saw there were many more swords and scabbards in the sack.

"LOOK!" boomed Arthur, and for a horrible moment Pat was sure he'd been spotted. But, as he raised his head, he saw the king was pointing to the middle of the lake. Sir Percival clutched hold of Merlin, who nodded to himself as the water began to bubble . . .

And suddenly, to Pat's amazement and alarm, a slender arm clad in shimmering white fabric reached up from the black depths of the lake, holding a sword aloft. Gulping hard, Pat looked down at the sword he had pulled from the sack. It seemed identical to the one now pointing up from the water.

"She rises!" bellowed Merlin, almost losing his hat as he reared up in excitement.

"It is a lady!" squealed Sir Percival.

Merlin shook his long-horned head with a grim smile. "Not quite . . ."

Sure enough, as smoky clouds blew clear of the moon, Pat could see quite clearly that the arm reaching out of the lake was not that of a lady. It wasn't even human. It ended in a fearsome mechanical hoof. And, as the blonde-haired figure rose up from the water, her lacy veil could not hide her glowing yellow eyes any more than her smock could disguise her hefty, stainless-steel udder . . .

"Behold, the Heifer of the Lake!" the bull-wizard proclaimed.

"So *that's* a ter-moo-nette," Pat realized, his chest tightening with fright. "A *female* ter-moo-nator!"

Bo felt as though she was falling in slow motion – and then suddenly she found herself in a moonlit forest, still clutching the strange sword they had found in Merlin's room. The professor was standing right beside her. "Hey!" she grumbled. "That stupid F.B.I. transporter sent us out of the castle!"

"And well away from any witnesses, meaning that beefy baddie can come and go without anyone knowing . . ." McMoo peered about. "There must be another transporter around here that the ter-moo-nator uses to get *into* the castle. . . Aha!" He pointed to an identical box half-buried beside a tree. Bo leaned closer, waving her sword, but McMoo snatched it away. "Careful! I told you before, the transporters must be activated by F.B.I. technology – otherwise any passing humans could whisk themselves into Cow-me-lot by mistake."

"That thing's not technology," Bo argued. "It's just a sword."

"Is it?" McMoo studied the long, silver weapon. "I have a feeling there's more to this blade than meets the eye." He looked at Bo. "So! The question is, why did our ter-moo-nating friend set up a secret transporter link right outside Merlin's private rooms?"

Bo gasped. "I know! Because Merlin and the ter-moo-nator are one and the same! He dresses up as Merlin to trick Arthur, sneaks back to get changed in Merlin's bedroom, then zips off out here."

"Then why not hide the transporter

inside Merlin's room instead of leaving it on the landing?" McMoo pointed out. "And why bother to get changed at all?"

"Shhh," Bo whispered. "I think I just heard something."

McMoo cocked his head to listen.

"Hurr, hurr, hurr . . ." came a familiar chuckle, and a burly, bald-headed man gripping a cleaver shambled out from the trees ahead of them.

"Oh, no," groaned McMoo. "Not hopeless Henry on the hunt again . . ."

"Don't you talk about my husband like that, tin-features!" Bessivere Barmer burst out from the bushes behind them – holding a large axe!

"Go away," McMoo said firmly, raising the strange sword. "We don't want any trouble."

"Then you shouldn't have come trespassing on private property," Bessivere snarled. "This is our front garden!"

Bo groaned. "That must be another reason why the ter-moo-nator set up the portal here – so any investigating C.I.A. agents like us would get bashed by a butcher!"

"*Eek!*" Bessivere jumped in the air, and Henry looked even more dumbfounded than usual. "That cow talks!"

"Oh, Bo," McMoo sighed.

"Sorry, Prof," said Bo. "I forgot ringblenders translate cow-speak into human, even if we're *not* dressed up to look like people."

"It's that Merlin isn't it!" Bessivere wailed. "He's put a spell on her!" Then she recovered and raised her axe. "But

so long as she still tastes the same, who cares?"

McMoo raised the sword, but Bo shook her head. "It's all right, Professor." She put her hooves on her hips. "I can handle these two with one arm tied behind my back and my tail tied to my udder."

"Oh, really?" Bessivere smiled nastily. "Then we might just need a little extra help . . ." She let rip with an enormous whistle. In seconds, the dark forest was alive with heavy crashing noises!

Bo gulped as a swarm of at least forty hairy, sweaty men in white, bloodstained coats charged into the clearing, waving rocks and knives and spatulas.

"Unfortunately for you, little magic cow," growled Bessivère, "I'm hosting the Federation of British Master Butchers' annual gala dinner tonight!"

"Ah," said McMoo. "And of course, there's no beef to be had, is there?"

"Exactly!" fussed a short, greasy feller. "A butchers' banquet with no beef — it's a scandal!"

"And we've eaten everything else in the forest," another man complained. "We're down to roast rat and bluetit soup!"

"Barmer said she had friends coming," Bo remembered. "That's why she was out hunting earlier this evening."

The butchers gasped to hear her speak. And then they started to drool.

"A talking cow!" one man boggled. "Imagine what *that*'s going to taste like!"

"Yellow udder," noted another, sucking his spatula. "She must be corn fed."

"Luvverly!" A fat, hairy butcher stepped forward, clicking his knuckles. "Let's take care of the knight first . . ."

"They mean business, Bo," McMoo murmured. "And they're blocking our way back to the transporter."

Bo nodded as the men started to close

in. "There's too many to fight, even for me," she whispered. "I think it's time to make like a nose, Professor — and RUN!"

Chapter Seven

A CURIOUS QUEST

At Dozmary Pool — unaware of the danger facing Bo and the professor — Pat watched astounded as the ter-moo-nette began to wade out of the dark waters. She held a sword aloft in one hand, and wore another in a scabbard at her metal hip. Both were identical to the one Pat had found in the sack.

King Arthur and Sir Percival stared in amazement as the gleaming vision clanked closer. Merlin's lips twitched in a broad smile. "A fair cow in shining armour," the bull breathed. "A symbol that cows shall be *our* armour against the evil Moodrid."

At last, the ter-moo-nette reached the shore. "Greetings," she said in a high, grating voice. "I thought there might be more of you."

"Forgive me, great heifer," said Merlin, bowing his head so far his hat fell off. "In my eagerness to gaze upon you, I forgot to tell the king to bring as many knights as he could."

"But frankly," said Sir Percival, "now you've met me, the others will only come as a disappointment!"

"Hush, Percy," hissed King Arthur. Then he turned to the ter-moo-nette. "Merlin told us you wished to speak of a great quest?"

"That is correct," said the part-metal
moo-cow. "You must journey far and
wide on a quest for the finest, sweetest
tasting hay on the planet . . . a quest for
the *HAYLY* Grail!"

"Hurrah!" cried Sir Percival. "But . . . how will we know if we've found it?"

"Feed it to a cow," said the ter-moo-nette. "If the cow does a somersault, then you have truly found the grail."

"What rubbish," Pat murmured. "She's tricking them all! But why?"

The ter-moo-nette offered the sword she carried to Arthur. "Each knight who searches for the Hayly Grail must carry one of these special swords at all times, so the world shall know of their business. And the swords are named . . . 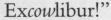 Ex*cow*libur!"

The king carefully took the silver blade. "Thank you, oh great heifer."

"Oooh!" said Sir Percival. "There's a cow's head carved into the hilt. That is divine!"

"Be sure to keep the sword's scabbard by your side." The heifer reached under her white smock and pulled out one for Arthur. "It will bring you . . . much luck on your travels."

I bet it won't! Pat thought, his heart starting to pound.

The ter-moo-nette handed a second sword and scabbard to Sir Percival. "Now, you must hurry and tell all the knights of Cow-me-lot of this quest. Let the word spread far and wide. All must gather in the courtyard at midday tomorrow, so that I may hand out Excowliburs to one and all . . ."

"I've got to do something," Pat fretted. "Oh, where are Bo and the professor? If only they were here!"

"One last thing, fair heifer." Merlin stepped closer to the unearthly cow. "In my dream, you said that if Arthur and his knights accept the quest and travel far in search of the hay, cows will never turn against us. Is that true?"

"Of course," the ter-moo-nette purred. "This quest will see the start of a great new age . . ."

Pat couldn't bear to stay silent any longer. "Yes – an age of evil cattle!" he yelled, jumping up. "Don't listen to her! She's tricking you all."

"Who dares spy on us?" King Arthur thundered.

The ter-moo-nette
swung round, her
yellow eyes like probing
spotlights. They fixed Pat
in their glare.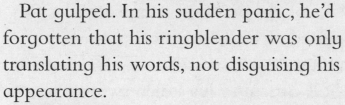

"It's another talking
cow!" cried Sir Percival.

Pat gulped. In his sudden panic, he'd
forgotten that his ringblender was only
translating his words, not disguising his
appearance.

"That is no cow . . ." Merlin reared up
onto his back legs to mirror Pat's own
pose. "It is a talking BULL! At last –
Moodrid himself has come to face me!"

He doesn't recognize me, thought Pat.
*I suppose that to humans, one cow looks a
lot like another by moonlight.* "I'm not
Moodrid!" he hollered.

"This bullock must be destroyed,"
droned the ter-moo-nette.

"It is *my* destiny to fight Moodrid,"
said Merlin, dropping back down onto

all fours. "It must be for this purpose
that my body was transformed – a duel
of might and moo-gic . . . to the death!"

With a bullish bellow of rage, Merlin
lowered his head so that the pointed
wizard's hat resembled a third horn
– and charged. King Arthur and Sir
Percival cheered and clapped and
shouted as his heavy hooves tore up
the turf.

Still clutching his stolen sword, Pat ran
for his life . . .

★ ★ ★

Deep in the dark forest beyond Cow-
me-lot, Professor McMoo and Bo were
running too. Unable to see far in the
blackness, McMoo was black and blue
inside his armour from crashing into
trees. But the butchers on their trail
seemed to know the forest far better.
They were gaining on the C.I.A. agents,
shouting and yelling with growing
excitement.

"I have to rest a moment," McMoo
panted, staggering to a stop. "This suit
weighs a ton!" Then he frowned. "Hold
on. Where's that light coming from?"

"It's coming from your sword!" Bo
pointed to the carved hilt. "It's just
the eyes in the cow face catching the
moonlight."

"I don't think so," said McMoo,
looking closely. "Those eyes are *glowing*!
I wonder how long they've been doing
that."

"Who cares?" She grabbed him by the hoof. "Come on, they're right behind us!"

McMoo lumbered round to see. "They *were* right behind us. But why has it suddenly gone so quiet?"

"Eh?" Bo listened — and noticed the sounds of pursuit had stopped. "Where did they go?"

Suddenly, a familiar sound floated from the forest: "*MOO!*"

"Professor, there's a cow out there!" Bo realized, starting forward. "If Barmer's butchers bump into it, the poor thing

won't stand a chance!"

"That didn't sound like a cow's moo to me . . ." Even as the professor spoke, a whole chorus of cattle calls sounded from the darkness. "Listen. It's like humans doing cow impressions!"

Cautiously, in the dim, dappled moonlight, McMoo and Bo made their way back to the clearing they had just crashed through. And there, down on all fours, were a number of butchers. They chewed on the grass, shuffling about on their hands and knees, mooing.

Bo's eyes narrowed. "What are they playing at?"

"Being cows, by the look of it," said McMoo, baffled.

The next moment, both of them jumped as Bessivere's head emerged from a nearby bush. "*Mooooo!*" She shuffled out on hands and feet, a big wad of grass hanging out of her mouth.

Henry was crawling right behind her. "Hurr-mooo," he said. "Moo-hurr-hurr-mooooooo . . ."

"This is weird," Bo concluded. "One moment they're chasing us like maniacs, the next they're acting like peaceful cows who'd never hurt a fly."

"They appear to be in a kind of

hypnotic state . . ." McMoo frowned. "I wonder how many others are being affected."

Then suddenly, the clatter of cracking branches and heavy footsteps carried through the darkness. "There's someone who isn't," Bo murmured nervously. "And they're approaching fast. Shall we get running again?"

"No, Bo." McMoo straightened up in his heavy armour. "There are too many unsolved mysteries in Arthur's kingdom. This time, we stay and fight!"

Chapter Eight

MERLIN RE-VEAL-ED!

"Give me the sword," Bo hissed. "I'll be better with it than you are!"

"You're probably right," McMoo agreed, passing it to her. He held his breath as whatever was racing towards them got closer and closer . . .

Until Pat came bursting from the bushes, a sword tucked under one arm. He skidded to a surprised stop.

"Little bruv!" Bo beamed.

"Pounding parsnips, am I ever glad to see you two." Pat staggered over to McMoo and Bo and leaned on them, panting for breath. "I've been running for ages. Merlin's chasing me! There

was this ter-moo-nette, see — a lady ter-moo-nator — dressed up as the Heifer of the Lake . . ."

"*What?*" Bo gasped.

"Slow down, Pat," McMoo urged him. "What's that sword you're holding?"

"The ter-moo-nette had a sack load of them, hidden in a monk's robes. I managed to get hold of one, it's called an Excowlibur . . ." He frowned as he saw the sword's twin clamped in Bo's hoof. "Hey, you've got one too!"

"Excowlibur, eh?" McMoo took Pat's sword and studied it. "And if those monk's robes are anything to go by, it sounds as though that ter-moo-*nette* is the one who visited Merlin in his private rooms . . ."

"She wants King Arthur and his knights to take the swords on a quest," explained Pat. "I tried to say she was tricking them, but then Merlin chased after me and—"

"*MOO!*" said Bessivere Barmer, as if annoyed by this interruption to her quiet grazing.

Pat stared round properly in the gloom. "Why are the barmy Barmers pretending to be cows? Who are all these smelly people eating grass—?"

"Time for a proper catch-up later," McMoo broke in, tossing Pat's sword into the forest. "Right now, we'd better think of a plan to deal with Merlin when he gets here—"

"I *am* here!" boomed Merlin, crashing into sight. He seemed short of breath and his wizard's hat was bent and askew. "Be warned, Sir Angus. This young bull you have brought to Cow-me-lot is

the enemy that I alone must face – the merciless Moodrid!"

"You can drop the act now, 'Merlin'," said McMoo gruffly.

Bo nodded. "We saw the ter-moo-nette visit you in your chambers."

"By my five balls of crystal!" Merlin gasped. "This cow speaks too!"

"Oh, give it a rest!" said Pat. "You tricked Arthur and his knights into coming to the lake so your mechanical missus could impress them – admit it."

"Tricked? How dare you!" Merlin stormed. "The heifer came to me in a dream, just as I said!"

Bo frowned. "Why are you even bothering to act like the real Merlin? We know you're an F.B.I. fake!"

"Or do we?" breathed McMoo. "Hang on one itty-bitty, cotton-picking moo here!" He turned to Bo. "We didn't see Merlin in his chambers, did we? Perhaps he *was* asleep when the ter-moo-nette visited. Just as he was asleep when he changed into a bull . . ."

"Oh, my sweet potatoes!" Pat pointed at Merlin's side. "Just look at that!"

By the lights of the jewels still aglow in Bo's borrowed sword, McMoo saw what he meant. "Well, well! Ran through some thorns on your way here, did you?"

Merlin frowned. "Well, yes, but I don't see—"

"The sneaky old codger!" Bo cried. "He *was* tricking us all along."

"I think it's Merlin who's been tricked," McMoo murmured.

Merlin glanced behind – and gasped in horror. A long, deep tear had opened up in his flank to reveal fabric

underneath – dark fabric patterned
with little moons and stars. "What is the
meaning of this?" he spluttered.

"It means, you're not really a bull at
all. You're a man, just as you've always
been!" McMoo grabbed hold of Merlin's
big bull's head and tugged with all his
might. With a loud tearing noise, it
ripped away to reveal the pale, startled
face of an old, wrinkled gentleman with
a white, flowing beard. "You see?" he
went on. "You've been wearing a highly
sophisticated fancy-dress costume from
the future."

"But it seemed so real!" Merlin stared down at his full bull bodysuit in shock. "This can't be!"

"Yes it can!" With a well-aimed swipe of her sword, Bo slashed the suit down the middle. It fell away to reveal a long, crumpled, smelly cloak underneath.

"*Ugh!*" Pat held his nose. "Merlin must have been stuck inside that costume for weeks . . ."

McMoo nodded grimly. "Just be glad he's wearing anything at all!"

The wizard still looked baffled, wiggling his hands and feet as if trying to convince himself he was indeed human. "But why would anyone want to make me think I had changed into a bull?"

"To make sure you took your visions seriously, I suppose," said McMoo. "You thought they were dreams – but really the ter-moo-nette's been sneaking into your room in person!"

"We followed you tonight, and saw her," Bo explained.

"Truly, the heifer's moo-gic is a powerful thing," said the woozy wizard. "I have been unfairly tricked!"

"It *had* to be a clever trick," said McMoo. "Because you're the smartest man alive in this time."

"Everyone listens to you, Merlin," Pat agreed. "King Arthur, his knights . . . They all believe you, whatever you say."

"And so they should!" Merlin told him sharply. "But you're right. Thanks to me, everyone is convinced that by being nice to cows we can stop merciless Moodrid from overthrowing our world."

"When in fact," came a high, robotic voice behind them, "your kindness to cows will *allow* me to overthrow your world . . ."

Pat, Bo, Merlin and McMoo turned to find the sinister, robed and hooded figure of the ter-moo-nette standing behind them – with a ray gun in her metal hoof.

"Puny, ignorant fools," she growled. "*I am Moodrid!*"

Chapter Nine

THE POWER OF EXCOWLIBUR

"Yak's spies must have got their wires crossed," McMoo said grimly. "They thought the F.B.I. was sending a deadly agent called Moodrid *and* a brand-new type of ter-moo-nator."

"Moodrid is my codename," the heavy-metal heifer explained. "It means Mechanical Ordeal Organizer – Damsel Revelling In Destruction."

"Catchy," said Pat.

"I suspected this bullock from the future would show you the truth, wizard," the ter-moo-nette went on. "But you must not be allowed to warn King Arthur."

"Vile trickster!" cried Merlin, lunging for the hooded figure. Calmly, she fired her gun at the ground just in front of him. A small explosion blew wet leaves up his cloak and sent him jumping back into Pat.

But while the metal cow was distracted, McMoo grabbed Bo's sword and held it in both hooves. "Put down your gun," he warned the ter-moo-nette. "Or I'll break this Excowlibur in half!"

Bo rolled her eyes. "Why should she care? She's got a sack of them!"

"But each one is a lot more than just a simple sword . . ." McMoo wobbled the blade threateningly. "Isn't it, Moodrid?"

The ter-moo-nette aimed her gun at Pat. "If you break it, *I* will break C.I.A. Agent Pat Vine."

Pat gulped. "I think I might break wind!"

"Hurt my brother," said Bo, "and I'll break *you* into tiny pieces!"

McMoo grinned. "What a pleasant conversation! Anything you'd like to break, Merlin?"

Merlin didn't answer. He was holding his head as though it ached, and Pat couldn't really blame him.

"Tell you what, ter-moo-nette," McMoo went on. "I won't hurt yours if you don't hurt mine. Just answer some questions — such as, what's so special about these swords, eh?"

The ter-moo-nette glared at him. "The Excowlibur weapons are hypno-swords," she grated. "They are programmed to send out a signal that hypnotizes the human mind. With one wave of my sword, I can make humans believe anything I choose."

"So *that's* how you made Merlin believe he was a bull and not a bloke in a costume!" McMoo looked down at the glowing eyes in the cow's face carved on the sword's hilt. "Hang on – it's working now, isn't it!"

The ter-moo-nette nodded. "Your clumsy handling must have set it off by mistake. It is transmitting a special pre-programmed hypnotic signal."

"So, when Bessivere Barmer and her butcher buddies came after us, they became hypnotized," McMoo realized. "Hypnotized into thinking they are cows . . ."

Bo nodded. "But it didn't work on us because we're cows already!"

"It's working on me!" Merlin clutched his head more tightly. "I can feel the hypnotic signal in my mind. I . . . can't . . . resist . . ." Suddenly, Merlin flopped down onto all fours with a loud "*MOOOOOO!*"

The professor stared in alarm – and
while his attention was taken, the ter-
moo-nette struck! She clobbered Pat
round the horns so he fell backwards
into Bo, and snatched the sword from
McMoo's grip at the same time.

"Do not move," Moodrid droned,
pointing her ray gun at the C.I.A.
agents as Merlin shuffled away on all
fours.

"Poor old Merlin," said Pat sadly.
"From costumed bull to make-believe
cow!"

"He has served his purpose," said

the metal agent. "Thanks to him,
King Arthur believed my story. The
knights of the Round Stable will
take my Excowlibur swords on their
hopeless quest, all around the world
— transmitting the hypnotic signal
wherever they go. Eventually, everyone
on the planet will come to think they
are a cow!"

Bo frowned. "But won't
the knights be hypnotized
too?"

"The swords' special
scabbards will protect the
knights and those close to them from
the hypnotic effect," the ter-moo-nette
explained. "But as the knights journey
onwards, those they leave behind will
soon fall under the hypnotic spell and
become human cows . . ." She cackled
suddenly with mechanical glee. "Right
around the world, they will do nothing
but moo and eat grass all day. And since

 humans cannot digest grass, they will waste away and perish – no matter how much they eat!"

McMoo turned up his nose. "That's the most revolting plan I have ever heard!"

"Thank you, Professor!" The ter-moo-nette fluttered her steel eyelids coyly. "You old smoothie! But it's no good trying to butter me up now." Her voice began to rise to an electronic shriek. "We shall rebuild the world with cattle in charge. Here in the sixth century, we shall create an evil-cow empire that will rule the planet for all time. Nothing can stop the F.B.I. . . . NOTHING!"

"Nice speech," said Pat, glowering. "But what happens to the three of us?"

The ter-moo-nette smiled. "I shall

keep you in my secret base as hostages in case of further C.I.A. interference."

"Cool," Bo whispered to Pat and McMoo. "We can jump her on the way there!"

"My secret base is actually one-point-seven metres away," Moodrid went on, pointing to a huge, hollow oak just behind them.

"Ah." McMoo glanced at Bo. "In that case . . ."

Bo turned and sprang into action, squirting a stream of milk at the ter-moo-nette's hoof which blasted the gun from her grip. But the F.B.I. agent retaliated with her own robotic udder.

It was like a fire hose going off!

A high-pressure jet of sour cream and runny butter struck Bo with punishing force and hurled her to the ground. "*Ugh!*" she spluttered. "Enough already!"

"Yes, you've made your point." McMoo sighed. "No more tricks, I

promise. We will come with you."

"Very well." The ter-moo-nette switched off the spray, picked up her fallen ray gun and gestured to the tree. "Now, move. In my haste to follow Merlin, I left some extra Excowliburs beside the lake. Once I have locked you away, I must retrieve them before appearing to Arthur's knights at noon . . ."

With Moodrid's gun aimed at their backs, McMoo and Pat helped up the spluttering Bo and half carried her into the tree.

Grazing and mooing peacefully in the breaking dawn, Merlin, Bessivere, Henry and the butchers barely noticed a thing . . .

Chapter Ten

FROM NOON TILL KNIGHT

No sooner did Pat find himself tied up in the ter-moo-nette's secret base, than he was racking his brains for a possible escape plan. But with Bo and the professor roped together too, and since the "secret base" was really more of a secret hole-in-the-ground-hidden-beneath-a-tree, he wasn't having much luck.

A single burning candle gave the only light in the place. Not that there was much to see except muddy walls, bits of tree root, a few boxes and the metal

hatch in the roof through which they had entered — now locked tight shut. Hours had crawled by slower than a one-legged tortoise with a stubbed toe, and Pat had lost all track of time. Could it be noon already? Was the ter-moo-nette's evil plan already underway?

"Well, this is nice," said Bo, still soggy and extremely grumpy. "I hope the C.I.A. send someone to help us soon."

"Even if they find us, they'll be too late." McMoo sighed. "There were loads of knights at the court of Camelot. By the end of today, they'll be scattered across Britain and heading overseas – turning people into cow-zombies without even knowing it."

Bo strained against her ropes. "There must be something we can do!"

"There is," came a muffled voice from above the roof. "Tell me how I can unlock this hidden hatchway and get you out!"

Pat gasped. "That sounds like . . ."

"Merlin!" McMoo grinned incredulously. "We thought you'd been hypnotized!"

"Am I not Merlin the Wise? Did you not show me the light of truth?" The wizard cleared his throat. "I'm just a bit embarrassed it took me a few hours to find it again . . ."

"Don't be," McMoo called to him. "Breaking the F.B.I.'s hypnosis was an impressive feat."

"I wish his feet were impressive enough to stamp a hole in that hatch," said Bo. "But it's solid metal."

"Speaking of metal, I have found one of the heifer's swords," Merlin went on.

"That must be the one I took away with me," Pat realized. "You threw it into the forest, Professor – remember?"

McMoo nodded. "And I remember that the ter-moo-nette's transporter device is programmed to respond to F.B.I. technology, so . . ."

"Perhaps the entrance to her secret base is too!" Pat concluded.

Bo raised his voice. "Have a good prod about with that sword, Beardie – double-quick!"

They heard clanging and battering as Merlin brought the sword down on the hatch. Pat held his breath and crossed his hooves and tail, and even managed to cross one of his ears, which wasn't easy . . .

And suddenly, the hatch swept open!

"It worked!" McMoo cried. "Thank you, Merlin."

"It is good to fight moo-gic with moo-gic!" said Merlin, scrambling down into the room. For an old man he was very spry, and his green eyes sparkled as he cut through Pat's ropes, then Bo's and then McMoo's. "But the question arises, my friends – what are we to do now?"

"First off, let's have a proper look inside this sword." McMoo glanced

around the ter-moo-nette's hidey-hole. "Somewhere about here there should be some tools . . ."

Pat opened one of the boxes he'd seen. It was full of complicated bric-a-brac. "This stuff any good?"

"Well spotted, Pat!" McMoo rummaged inside, grabbed a screwdriver and set about the sword in Merlin's hands. "So, tell me, great wizard — how did you find us?"

"I'm magic." Merlin smiled, his eyes twinkling. "And I'm also quite good at following tracks in the ground!" Bo smiled back. "You're even better at telling King Arthur what to do. We must get you back to Cow-me-lot so you can tell him how that robotic ratbag has tricked everyone."

"You speak wisely, talking cow," Merlin declared. "But will the heifer not use her great moo-gic to silence us? I may not have the strength to escape her spells a second time."

"That's a point," said McMoo, frowning. "She must be able to switch on the Excowliburs by remote control whenever she's ready."

"If only we had one of the special scabbards, we could block the hypnotic signal!" Pat sighed.

"At least we've got a sword," said McMoo brightly, removing a panel to expose the wires and circuits within.

"You know, I think I have a plan – but it's riskier than shaving with a ter-moo-nator's toenail . . ."

"Whatever your plan, I fear it is too late." Merlin pointed up at the sky through the hatch. "Behold! The sun has risen high above the land. Only minutes remain until noon!"

Noon found King Arthur waiting for the heiffer to appear in Cow-me-lot's courtyard. Sir Percival stood at his side, and a crowd of 101 other knights – all those he'd been able to round up overnight – stood about heroically. The rest of the courtyard was clogged with curious nobles, ladies, men at arms and servants – as well as dozens of Cow-me-lot's cattle.

Arthur sighed and looked around for the thousandth time. "I do wish Merlin would return. He's been gone for ages."

"He'll show up, sire," said Sir Percival.

"And when he does, I bet he'll have
sorted out that wicked Moodrid
for good." He smiled down at the
Excowlibur in his hand. "You know,
my reflection really is extra-pretty in
this sword!"

King Arthur rolled his eyes. "I say!" he called to a man-at-arms beside the drawbridge. "The Heifer of the Lake should arrive at any moment. Lower that thing so she can get inside . . ."

"I am ALREADY inside!" came a loud, commanding voice from behind him.

A collective gasp went up from the gathered crowds. Hundreds of heads turned, cows mooed as if in amazement and a wave of excited chatter swept through the courtyard.

Arthur now found himself right at the back of the crowd and unable to see a thing. "Clear a path!" he boomed.

The startled audience of knights,
commoners and cattle began shifting
about to create a gangway through the
middle of the courtyard. Then Arthur
gasped, and his knights nearly swooned,
as the cow-like creature they had seen
the night before was revealed – a vision
in white silk and steel. Her long blonde
hair reached down to the large pile
of swords she carried in her arms, and
yellow eyes glowed behind her veil.

"Great heifer!" Arthur dropped to his knees, and his assembled knights bowed down low. "Do you bring us good tidings of brave Merlin?"

"Merlin has not yet caught up with Moodrid," the Heifer of the Lake explained, striding towards them in six-inch steel heels. "He is still chasing the evil bullock."

"Still? Half a day later?" King Arthur raised his eyebrows. "My, the old boy's got some stamina!"

"Enough talk of Merlin," the heifer  announced, towering over Arthur. "It is more urgent than ever that your knights begin their quest for the Hayly Grail at once."

Arthur raised his Excowlibur sword aloft. "We are ready and willing!"

"And terribly excited," added Sir Percival.

"We shall journey to the four corners of the earth in search of the finest hay, fair lake-cow!" called another knight.

"I shall cross rivers of fire and chasms of doom to fetch it," said yet another.

"I shall cross them faster," a more competitive knight declared. "Plus, I will probably slay a dragon too."

"I will *definitely* slay a dragon," said Sir Percival.

"All right, I get the idea," rumbled the Heifer of the Lake. "Just remember, to ensure good fortune on your quest, you must take my special swords everywhere you go and wear the lucky scabbard—"

"DON'T LISTEN TO HER!"

King Arthur started at the familiar

voice behind him, as the crowds gasped and squealed in amazement.

"You!" squawked the Heifer of the Lake.

Arthur turned to find Merlin standing in the courtyard entrance – back in his old, familiar form of a bearded, mussed-up old man! "Merlin!" he cried with delight. Beside the wizard stood the mysterious milk-white knight, Sir Angus – but of his two cows there was no sign.

"How did you get here?" the heifer growled.

"We have used your own moo-gic against you, vile cow of evil," Merlin shouted back. "And now . . . let the final battle commence!"

Chapter Eleven

SIGNAL OF DOOM

Professor McMoo watched Arthur as he rushed over, grabbed Merlin in a hug, sniffed him, almost choked and quickly put him down again.

"You are no longer a bull, Merlin," the king observed in wonder. "What does this mean?"

"It means we have all been tricked by that lying rat of a cow!" cried Merlin, as further gasps echoed around the courtyard. "*She* was the evil Moodrid all along, Arthur! Her quest is a mockery.

She plans to use the knights of the Round Stable to destroy the world!"

A heavy silence settled over the courtyard as the news sank in.

"Destroying the world isn't very chivalrous," squeaked Sir Percival. "I'd sooner not!"

"Order your knights to capture that heifer, Your Majesty," McMoo urged Arthur. "Before she can act against us."

"Capture a damsel?" King Arthur looked shocked. "Isn't that against the rules?"

"You are all welcome to try," growled the ter-moo-nette. She started pulling Excowliburs from their scabbards and tossing them to the other knights assembled in the crowd. "I'll even give you extra weapons to make it easy . . ."

"Come on, Pat and Bo, get a shift on," breathed McMoo. Then he called to the knights: "Throw down those swords, all of you! She's up to something!"

"Me, Professor?" She smiled and produced a remote control from beneath her smock. "Why, whatever can you mean?" She pressed a button. Suddenly, the eyes in the cow-crafted sword hilts started to glow with evil energy.

"It's no good trying to hypnotize everyone," McMoo warned, advancing on the ter-moo-nette. "You've brought too many of your special scabbards with you. They'll block the hypnotic signal, remember?"

"Not if I turn that signal up to *eleven*!" hissed the ter-moo-nette, turning a dial on the remote. A sinister hum filled the air. Crackles of power spat from the Excowlibur blades, and the eyes in the hilts grew ever brighter. The knights

gasped in horror, and the damsels in the crowd – not wishing to show up the knights – duly started to scream and faint. Sir Percival yelped as his scabbard exploded. Arthur's shattered into pieces, hurling him to the ground. McMoo stared round in alarm as the sword sheaths started blowing apart all over the place.

As the scabbards were destroyed, so the full power of the ter-moo-nette's hypnotic signal coursed through the courtyard and beyond, into the cobbled streets of Cow-mc-lot. Nobles and knights, servants and soldiers, all were clutching their ears and starting to moo. One by one, they dropped to all fours, while real cattle ran for cover in confusion.

"Hold on to your mind, sire!" Merlin beseeched King Arthur. "You must hold on!"

But Arthur was already falling to his

knees. He shuffled up to a nearby dairy cow and started chewing her grass.

McMoo lunged for the ter-moo-nette's remote control, but she stopped him with a blast of rancid yoghurt from her automated udder. "Stop this!" he spluttered. "You can't turn these knights into human cows — you need them to help you conquer the world, remember?"

"And so they shall." The ter-moo-nette gave Merlin a yoghurt squirt too, and with a cry he slipped to the cobblestones. "I will hypnotize the people of Cow-me-lot again and convince them that none of this ever happened. I will repair the scabbards, and recapture Pat and Bo Vine, wherever they have gone."

"Quite a to-do list," said McMoo.

"*Then* I shall appear to King Arthur and his knights once again. And this time, all will go smoothly." She loomed over McMoo and Merlin. "My plans *will* succeed, Professor. But now, for putting me to so much trouble, you and the wizard must be ter-moo-nated!"

Choking on yoghurt and too slippery to stand, with hundreds of moos echoing in his ears, the professor watched helplessly as Moodrid picked up a fallen Excowlibur sword in her free hoof and raised it higher . . . *higher* . . .

CLANG!

The next moment, a hurled shield smashed the weapon and the remote control from the ter-moo-nette's metal grip. The gadgets fell into a pool of bubbling yoghurt, and started to smoke and spark.

"Yes!" cheered the professor.

"NOOOO!" Moodrid warbled. She ducked down and started scrabbling for the slippery sword – and McMoo grinned to see Bo doing a victory dance behind her.

"Pretty cool throw, eh, Professor?" Bo yelled.

"I certainly got a kick out of it . . ." McMoo lashed out with one armoured hoof and booted the ter-moo-nette over into her own vile dairy slime. "And what do you know, so did she!"

The remote control was starting to melt. "Power levels too high," gasped the ter-moo-nette, searching for the device. "Yoghurt levels too toxic. Must deactivate before . . ."

"Too late!" cried McMoo as the remote began to jump about like a smoking steel firecracker. "It's going to blow!"

"So it seems, Professor." The ter-moo-nette's eyes glowed nastily. "And the resulting explosion will destroy you!"

Chapter Twelve

A KIND OF MOO-GIC

"Destroy the prof? Not if I can help it!" Bo wrenched the metal breastplate from the nearest knight, jumped onto it and used it as a surfboard to skim across the pool of yoghurty slime at incredible speed. "Grab hold, Professor!"

Clutching onto Merlin's cloak, McMoo reached out with his other hoof for Bo. She snatched him and the wizard to safety – just as Moodrid's remote burst apart, belching purple flames and thick green smoke.

Back on dry cobbles, McMoo staggered to his feet with a very groggy Merlin.

"Those were two excellent rescues, young cow," the wizard muttered.

"Yes, thanks, Bo." McMoo pretended to frown. "But did you have to leave them *both* to the very last minute?"

"Don't blame *me*!" Bo grinned. "That job you gave us took longer than you thought it would. In fact, I had to leave Pat to finish up while I hopped into the transporter. I had a feeling you might need me."

"You will both need an *ambulance*!" came an angry whine behind them. As the green smoke blew away on the breeze, the scorched, sticky and soot-blackened ter-moo-nette came into sight. She had lost her wig and her white dress was filthy.

140

"Look what you've done to my swords!"

Merlin marvelled as sparking Excowliburs all around the courtyard began to drip and dwindle like silver ice-lollies left out in the sun. "They're melting!"

"Their circuits are overloading," McMoo realized. "Moodrid must have boosted the hypnotic signal *too* much – and without the remote she can't turn it down again."

"Not fair!" warbled Moodrid. "With the swords destroyed, the hypnotic effect will soon fade. My plans are ruined!"

"Good," snapped Merlin.

"That's better than I dared hope for," McMoo agreed.

"And it gets even better!" Pat shouted, standing in the gateway to the courtyard.

"Little bruv!" Bo waved. "You made it.

Did you finish the job?"

Pat glanced behind him and smiled. "Oh, yes. We can get her now . . ."

"You think that the four of you can beat an armour-plated, computer-brained, nuclear-uddered ter-moo-nette?" The half-metal monster sneered. "I am Moodrid, Organizer of Ordeals! I revel in destruction . . . and I shall crush you like croutons beneath my steel stilettos!"

"If there really *were* only four of us, perhaps you could try." Pat took a step clear of the gateway. "But look who's just joined us in Cow-me-lot thanks to your handy transporter . . ."

The ter-moo-nette froze in sudden alarm as dozens and dozens of dirty, hairy butchers came charging into the courtyard, led by Henry and Bessivere Barmer!

"There's the metal cow!" bellowed Bessivere. "Get her, boys, and see how many dents you can give her!"

"Stay back!" squawked the ter-moo-nette. She raised her gun, but didn't know where to aim it first. Suddenly, a well-aimed cleaver jarred the weapon from her grip.

"Hurr! Hurr!" Henry chortled. "*Got* hurr!"

Merlin gave him a thumbs-up. "Good shot!"

"*Eeeeek!*" The ter-moo-nette was sent staggering backwards as dozens of clomping great butchers started grabbing for her switches and swiping at her armour. "Unhand me, humans! Release meeeeee . . ."

Pat came rushing over to join McMoo, Bo and Merlin. "Your plan worked, Professor!"

"Of course it did!" said McMoo. "You saw me reverse the circuits in that sword that Merlin found so that it sent out an *anti*-hypnotic signal. All you had to do was wave the sword around in front of those butchers to break their spell and produce an instant angry mob! What could have gone wrong with that?"

"It took ages!" Pat complained. "Bessivere and her mates have hardly got three brain cells to rub together!

It's just a good job their time as human cows has put them off eating *real* cows like Bo and me."

"Yeah – lucky for them!" Bo declared. "Even luckier, Bessivere jumped at the chance of getting revenge on the metal cow who made her miss her big gala dinner – just as you guessed she would, Professor."

"It was a remarkable plan." Merlin clapped McMoo on the back. "Truly, Professor, you are almost as wise as I am."

McMoo smiled. "You know, there aren't many people I'd let get away with a comment like that, Merlin – but you're one of them!"

"Never mind the congratulations," said Bo. "Let's see if Bessivere's rabble needs a hand with old iron-knickers over there!"

But it was clear that no help was required. The cheering, jeering butchers had lifted the battered ter-moo-nette into the air and were pulling her in all directions. "You've ruined my bodywork!" the metal madam shrieked over the hubbub. "*And* you've broken one of my heels."

"Throw her in the moat!" Bessivere yelled.

"No, don't! My waterproof coating has rubbed off!" The ter-moo-nette hastily pulled a silver platter from under her tattered smock.

Merlin sneered. "A shield won't save you, Moodrid!"

"It's not a shield." Pat sighed. "It's an F.B.I. portable time machine. She's going to get away!"

"Mission abort!" the ter-moo-nette droned, fading in a haze of fetching pink smoke. "Abort! Retreat! Mission aborrrrrrrt . . ."

Bo started forward, but the professor held her back. "No, let her go," he said. "I think there's been enough fighting here today."

"I guess," Bo grumbled. "But I have a feeling we'll be meeting that ter-moo-nette again . . ."

The butchers stared about in confusion as their victim vanished. Bessivere stamped over. "Oi! Where did that rotten tin cow go?"

"I'm not sure," McMoo admitted. "But she won't be back in a hurry – thanks to the lesson you taught her."

"Well, I've learned a

lesson too," Bessivere declared. "Grass is *yummy*, even if it's no good for you! I'm going to organize a jolly butchers' outing around the world, trying to find the tastiest type there is . . ."

Pat raised his eyebrows. "A quest for the *Grassy* Grail?"

"Right. Get that drawbridge down, Henry," bawled Bessivere, shoving her husband on ahead. "Then let's hit the road."

"I hope that's all she'll be hitting for a while," said McMoo, watching them go.

Bo grinned. "Good riddance!"

"Ohhhhh . . ." King Arthur was struggling to his feet, surrounded by dazed damsels and puzzled-looking knights. "What happened?" He looked down grimly at the stinky yellow puddle at his feet. "It must have been one heck of a party!"

"Someone's taken my breastplate!" Sir Percival was blushing scarlet, covering

his naked chest with both hands. "Help!"

"Here, have this helmet I found," Bo offered – and placed it back to front over the vain knight's head, to much applause from those waking up nearby.

"Camelot can return to normal at last," Merlin said happily. "Though I think we'll keep the cows around – in honour of the three brave cattle who saved us all."

"*Three?*" McMoo frowned. "You mean . . . you know I'm not a human knight?"

"That enchanted ring you wear

through your nose is most fetching, my friend." Merlin smiled warmly. "Professor, my eyes have been opened to the truth once more — and thanks to you, they shall stay that way."

Bo gave the old man a fond lick. "See ya, Beardie!"

"It was an honour to meet you," said Pat. "Good luck cleaning up around here, Merlin!" McMoo beamed at the old man. "I'd love to stay a while, but we'd better be off — I can hear a cup of tea brewing in the twenty-sixth century . . ."

"I shall take care of everything with my great magic," Merlin assured them, a twinkle in his eye. "And a little *moo-gic* thrown in for good measure!"

Exhausted but happy, McMoo, Pat and
Bo slipped away through the ter-moo-
nette's transporter and disconnected it
behind them. Then they trudged back to
the Time Shed.

"I hope we've heard the last of
moo-gic in the Dark Age," declared
the professor. "But I'm glad the tales
of Merlin, Arthur and all his knights
will continue to thrill audiences right
through history."

Pat nodded. "Even if it turns out the
storytellers got one or two of the details
wrong!"

With the Time Shed's engines now
working smoothly at full power, it didn't
take long for McMoo and his friends
to return to C.I.A. Headquarters in
the twenty-sixth century. The battered
old craft arrived in a blur of light and
creaking timber. But Yak, Dandi and
the rest of the staff hardly noticed. They

were too busy laughing at something on the P.O.O. scanner.

"Hey, what's going on, Yakeroo?" Bo demanded.

"Yes!" McMoo looked peeved. "We've saved the world, kept history on the right track – and there's not even a fresh cuppa waiting now we're back!"

"Sorry, team," Yak told them with a snigger. "You did a great job. And you'll be pleased to know that you've got a holiday coming up on your farm."

"Well, a holiday from Bessie Barmer, anyway." Dandi hit the rewind button beneath, and the images wound backwards. "While you were away, Bessie finally removed that pickaxe stuck in the concrete . . ."

She pressed play – and there on the screen was the twenty-first-century Bessie wrestling with a stout wooden pick handle. "Come on," the huge woman growled. "If King Arthur could pull the sword from the stone, I can do this. I am the once and future queen of farms . . ." Biceps the size of badgers sprang up on her arms as she strained with all her strength . . . "Yes . . . YES . . . YES!"

Incredibly, she lifted both the pickaxe and the block of concrete high into the air.

Then the concrete fell off and landed on her head.

"*OOOF!*" Bessie yelled, and fell face-first into the mud.

"*Ouch!*" Pat winced. "That's got to hurt."

"She'll be fine, I'm afraid!" Dandi told him. "A slight concussion, a week's rest at her sister's and she'll be back again to bug you."

"Then let's get back and make the most of a week off," Bo suggested.

"Once I've repaired the costume cupboard you mean!" McMoo reminded her. "And once we've picked up a stash of Yak's special-blend future tea bags . . ."

"I've sorted out a year's supply," Yak told him, handing over a huge pile. "You've earned it."

"'A year's supply!" McMoo's eyes were on stalks.

Bo looked at Pat. "That's going to last about three days."

"At the most!" McMoo joyfully

threw a hoof-ful of tea bags into the air. "But now we've found the *high-tea* grail, we're bound to be off on another C.I.A. quest very soon. Until then, it's "thank you . . . and good *knight!*"

THE END

COMING SOON!

Join the Cows In Action on their brand-new adventure!

Join the gang as they travel back to Victorian London where a mysterious, evil Cow of Doom is committing a string of terrible moo-ders.

Who will be next? How are the F.B.I involved? And can the C.I.A put history back on track once again . . . ?

Find out in the

THE VICTORIAN MOO-DERS

by Steve Cole

ISBN: 978 1 862 30883 1

COWS IN ACTION
THE UDDERLY MOOVELLOUS JOKE BOOK
by Steve Cole

What goes, 'oom, oom'?
A cow walking backwards!

What do you get if you sit under a cow?
A pat on the head!

With the F.B.I. working on a joke so funny it's deadly,
McMoo, Pat and Bo set out on their most hilarious

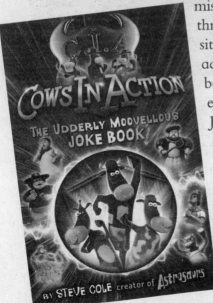

mission yet ... They travel
through time, revisiting the
sites of their most exciting
adventures, in search of the
best - and worst - jokes
ever ...
Jam-packed full of great
gags, witty wisecracks
and perfect puns, this
Udderly Moovellous
C.I.A. Joke Book will
have you chuckling and
chortling for hours!

ISBN: 978 1 862 30882 4

Join the C.I.A. on their first adventure!

THE TER-MOO-NATORS
by Steve Cole

IT'S 'UDDER' MADNESS!

Genius cow Professor
McMoo and his trusty
sidekicks, Pat and Bo,
are the star agents of
the C.I.A. – short for
COWS IN ACTION!
They travel through
time, fighting evil bulls
from the future and
keeping history on
the right track . . .

When Professor
McMoo invents a brilliant
TIME MACHINE, he and his friends are soon
attacked by a terrifying TER-MOO-NATOR - a
deadly robo-cow who wants to mess with the past
and change the future! And that's only the start of an
incredible ADVENTURE that takes McMoo, Pat and
Bo from a cow paradise in the future to the SCARY
dungeons of King Henry VIII . . .

It's time for action. COWS IN ACTION

ISBN: 978 1 862 30189 4

THE PIRATE MOO-TINY

by Steve Cole

OX MARKS THE SPOT!

Genius cow Professor McMoo and his trusty sidekicks,
Pat and Bo, are star agents of
the C.I.A. – short for COWS
IN ACTION! They travel
through time, fighting evil
bulls from the future and
keeping history on the right
track . . .

In 1718, robotic danger
HAUNTS the seven seas
. . . Posing as a pirate, a
TER-MOO-NATOR
is capturing ships in the
Caribbean. But why?
And what terrible
treasure is he hiding on
SPOOKY Udderdoom
Island? McMoo, Pat and Bo set
sail on a big, BUCCANEERING adventure to find
answers before pirate BULLS take over the world ...

It's time for action. COWS IN ACTION

ISBN: 978 1 862 30541 0

ALSO AVAILABLE BY STEVE COLE ...

Meet the Astrosaurs!

RIDDLE OF THE RAPTORS

BLAST OFF!

Teggs is no ordinary dinosaur – he's an ASTROSAUR! Captain of the amazing spaceship DSS *Sauropod*, he goes on dangerous missions and fights evil - along with his faithful crew, Gypsy, Arx and Iggy!

When a greedy gang of meat-eating raptors raid the *Sauropod* and kidnap two top athletes, Teggs and his crew race to the rescue. But there's more to the raptors' plot than meets the eye. Can Teggs solve their rascally riddle in time?

Collect your very own Astrosaurs cards! Included in the back of each book.

ISBN: 978 0 099 47294 0

Join the **Astrosaurs** on their
brand–new adventure . . .

THE DREAMS OF DREAD
by Steve Cole

IT'S DINO-MITE!

Teggs is no ordinary
dinosaur - he's an
ASROSAUR! Captain
of the amazing
spaceship DSS
Sauropod, he goes on
dangerous missions
and fights evil
– along with his
faithful crew, Gipsy,
Arx and Iggy!

Teggs and
the gang find
themselves trapped in a deadly
dream world! Here they are forced to face the
revolting raptors, dangerous dung-demons and scary
sabre-toothed bananas of their nightmares. Can they
escape back to reality, or will the dreams of dread keep
them prisoners for all time . . . ?

ISBN: 9781862305458